# TURKEY'S
# Thanksgiving Adventure

By **Clay Sproles**

Illustrations by **Lamont Russ**

Every book starts as an idea from one person,
but it takes several people to see it through to the end.

A Special Thanks
to Rayne Chase, Ellie Firestone, and Lamont Russ

Text copyright 2019 by Clay Sproles
Illustrations copyright 2019 by Clay Sproles

Summary: Illustrations and rhyming text about the funny antics of a turkey
trying to avoid being the main course on Thanksgiving.

First Edition

ISBN: 978-1-7334195-6-7

Cats Corner
Publishing

It was Thanksgiving's eve when the turkey got wise;
He heard the old farmer's wife sharpening her knives
He didn't want to be eaten. He wanted to stay!
To survive this Thanksgiving, he had to hide away.

The turkey tried to hide with
the ducks in the pond,
But of swimming and quacking
he wasn't too fond.

He tried to hide with the
pigs in their muddy sty,
But he couldn't stand the filth,
so he told them goodbye.

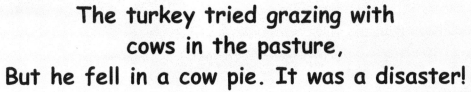

The turkey tried grazing with
cows in the pasture,
But he fell in a cow pie. It was a disaster!

He hopped over the fence, into the goat's pen,
But they were too loud, so he jumped again.

As his options grew to be fewer and fewer,
Our brave poultry hero grew bluer and bluer

The turkey paced back and forth,
and clucked as he went.
His life on the farm, he began to lament.

But the fowl was surely not one to give in.
One solution remained; he had to get thin.

The turkey was focussed on his thighs and his rump.
He began working out so he wouldn't look plump.

He did push-ups and sit-ups and pull-ups, and then
He sighed and did everything over again.

After exercising, the turkey was pooped.
He'd get back to it after a nap in his coop.

But just as the turkey closed his beady eyes,
He heard a noise, and woke up in surprise.

There stood the farmer, in overalls clad.
He said, "Don't worry, Turkey.
This news isn't bad."

The farmer tossed feed on the ground and said with a leer, "Eat up, turkey, so you'll grow bigger for next year!"

# Thank You!

If you enjoyed this book,
Please take a minute
to write an honest review

# Other Books by this Author

## Can You Hear The Diggers?

Is a rhyme that will take you on a trip to the construction site. An engaging story for kids to read along as the big machines RUMBLE, BUZZ, and CRASH their wav around!

## Snow Way Out

When a Blizzard hits the North Pole on Christmas Eve, Santa's sleigh gets stuck and in order to be able to deliver presents the Elves and Santa must find a way to free it

## Monster Bash

Dracula, the Wolf-Man and all of their monster friends find children dressed up for Halloween freighting so what do they do? Have a party a real Monster Bash!

## The Littlest Ghost

The little ghost doesn't want to miss out on all the candy, so he comes up with a genius plan. A costume that will hide his ghostly appearance, he will dress up as as GHOST!

CPSIA information can be obtained
at www.ICGtesting.com
Printed in the USA
LVHW070303071222
734277LV00009B/224

9 781733 419567